D1195436

The Little RED BUS

by 'Miss Read'

Illustrated by JENNETTA VISE

HOUGHTON MIFFLIN COMPANY

NEW YORK · ATLANTA · GENEVA, ILL · DALLAS · PALO ALTO

This is a bus.

It is shiny and red.

It stands every night
In this very big shed.

Now this man is Fred.
He comes every day
To drive the red bus
To town far away.

Now one night, when Fred
Was lying in bed,
And the shiny red bus
Was at rest in the shed,

THE SNOW CAME —— so fast
That, by the next day,

Poor Fred had to dig
To his bus, all the way.

He got in his bus
And he said: "We must go
To town with the people ——
Snow or no snow!

Up over the hill
And then we run down.
The people are waiting
To go into town!"

But the shiny red bus
Found the hill very steep,
And it could not go on
For the snow was too deep.

"Let's give you a push
Up this steep hill," said Fred,
And he pushed and he pushed
Till his face was quite red.

But the shiny red bus
Was stuck fast in the snow
On the side of the hill —
And it just could not go.

The people were waiting
Not far away.
"Now where is the bus?
We shall be late today!"

"I must do my shopping,"
Said fat Mrs.Bly,
"I want fish for my cat
And some plums for a pie."

"And we want plums too,"
Said Betty to Pat.
"And ribbon,"said Polly,
"To trim my best hat."

But the shiny red bus
Was still stuck in the snow
On the side of the hill ——
And it just could not go.

Just then came a postman.
"Can I help?" he said,
So the two pushed and pushed
Till their faces were red.

But the shiny red bus
Was still stuck in the snow
On the side of the hill ——
And it just could not go.

And then came a farmer.
"Can I help?" he said,
So the three pushed and pushed
Till their faces were red.

18

But the shiny red bus
Was still stuck in the snow
On the side of the hill ——
And it just could not go.

And then came a milkman.
"Can I help?" he said,
So the four pushed and pushed
Till their faces were red.

But the shiny red bus
Was still stuck in the snow
On the side of the hill ——
And it just could not go.

The milkman, the farmer,
The postman and Fred,
All looked at the bus
In its deep snowy bed.

"We must have more help,"
Said the milkman,

"I KNOW!
My horse could help pull
This bus out of the snow!"

They tied the good horse
To the bus with a rope.
"You pull while we push,
And we'll shift it, we hope."

The milkman, the farmer,
The postman and Fred,
All pushed at the back
Till their faces were red.

And the horse pulled in front,
With a puff and a blow ——

And the bus slowly came
From its bed in the snow.

They pushed and they pulled
To the top of the hill.
"Well done, horse!" they said,
When at last he stood still.

They gave him a pat.
"Without him, I know,"
Said Fred, "my red bus
Would still be in the snow."

Fred got in his bus.
"Thank you, friends," he called down,
And they all waved goodbye
As he drove off to town.

"Hooray! Here it comes!
There's the bus! And there's Fred!

We <u>can</u> go to town
After all!"people said.

"I'm sorry I'm late,"
Said Fred, "but you see
We have had an adventure,
My red bus and me."

And he told them about
The steep hill and the snow,
And the friends who had helped
When the bus could not go.

And you can be sure
That he told them —
        OF COURSE —
Of the friend who helped most —

The milkman's good horse.